*My deep thanks to Ulrike,
Sebastian, and Nina Buchholz,
Gisela Hofmann, Rolf Inhauser, Karin Rebke,
Hanno Rink, and Dirk Stempel*

This edition produced for Reading's Fun Ltd.

For Imke

Quint Buchholz

Sleep Well, Little Bear

Translated from the German by Peter F. Neumeyer

❧ ❧ ❧

Farrar Straus Giroux

NEW YORK

In the evening, the little bear took off his apple trousers
and put on his star pajamas.
He had heard a long good-night story.
He had said a small prayer.
He had hummed along with a little sleep song.
He had gotten five kisses.

But he still needed a drink of water from the blue cup,
because suddenly he was very thirsty,
just like he was every evening.
Then he had to put on his red sleeping socks,
because he had forgotten them.
Then he wanted someone to blow warm air under
the covers, because he felt so cold.

And only then could the light be turned out in his room.

It's all quiet now.
But the little bear is not tired.

And when little bears are not tired,
they scramble quietly out of their beds
and build themselves a staircase . . .

. . . to where the moon floats in the heavens
like a great round lantern, shining softly on the meadows,
on the house, on the trees, on the river,
and on the whole world.

It's cooler outside now.
The ducks are still taking a bath in the river.
Sometimes, in the silence,
you can hear the frogs croaking.

On the dock, a shirt blows in the evening breeze.
It had been the sail for a boat, in the afternoon,
when the little bear was a pirate.
And the shoe box was the treasure chest.

Next door lives old Mrs. Rose.
She had worked in her garden all afternoon.
She had dug and hoed and pruned and watered.
And while she worked,
she told stories to her flowers.

The little bear often visits Mrs. Rose.
He listens to her stories. Sometimes he helps
with his yellow shovel.

He can see from his window that
old Mrs. Rose has fallen asleep in her chair.
She was that tired.

In the meadow, at the edge of the forest, stands the birdman.
Last fall, the children made him out of odds and ends.
Now, when they come to play in his meadow,
they put fresh flowers or grasses in his hat.

The little bear gave the birdman his wooden car
with the red wheels.

There's a big circus tent in the next town.
Today, when the little bear went on a shopping trip,
he watched the circus people for a while.
He saw painted wagons, a man on stilts,
a woman selling cotton candy, a tiny pony,
and a great brown bear.

Now the show is finished, the crowd has gone home,
and the circus people have climbed into their wagons.

In the evening quiet,
the clown is playing a sleep song
on his violin for the baby elephant.

From time to time, late in the evening,
a barge goes down the river.
Maybe it is going to the nearest port;
maybe out to the great ocean.

The little bear sees the lights and hears,
very softly, the chugging of the engines.

A balloon with a letter hovers over the meadow.
It has traveled on a long, long journey.
And soon it's going to land.

Who is the letter for?
Maybe the little bear will find out.
Maybe tomorrow morning,
after he's had his sleep.

Tomorrow, the little bear will be a pirate once again,
and go sailing across the stormy seas with his captain.
They'll explore distant lands,
and they'll find a mysterious treasure chest.

The little donkey might visit tomorrow.
They'll go see old Mrs. Rose and help with the garden.

And then they'll go on an outing to the birdman's meadow.
It's wonderfully warm in the sun,
and sometimes the wagon goes terribly fast.

But what if the sun doesn't come out tomorrow?
What if it's raining tomorrow?

Then the little bear will scoot quickly to the barn
and clamber up to the loft.
Because the loft is his lair.
Up there, he has collected lots of things—
including a clay flute on which he can play his songs.

How cozy it is, sitting there all dry.
Especially when you've got something good to eat.

Outside, it's pouring rain, and everything smells so fresh.

The little bear can't wait until tomorrow.

But now it's nighttime.
The little bear closes his eyes.
Then he hears music, playing softly somewhere.
It's the moon musicians, who roam about
in the night, playing their songs.
For the moon, for the children, and for little bears.

The moon is in the sky the whole night long.
It shines on the meadows, on the house, on the trees,
on the river, and on the whole world.

It shines through the window, too.

Sometimes the little bear gives the moon a good-night kiss . . .